THE VERY ITCHY BEAR

NICK BLAND

Scholastic Canada Ltd.

Toronto New York London Auckland Sydney
Mexico City New Delhi Hong Kong Buenos Aires

For Walter

Scholastic Canada Ltd.
604 King Street West, Toronto, Ontario M5V 1E1, Canada

Scholastic Inc.
557 Broadway, New York, NY 10012, USA

Scholastic Australia Pty Limited
PO Box 579, Gosford, NSW 2250, Australia

Scholastic New Zealand Limited
Private Bag 94407, Botany, Manukau 2163, New Zealand

Scholastic Children's Books
Euston House, 24 Eversholt Street, London NW1 1DB, UK

Library and Archives Canada Cataloguing in Publication

Bland, Nick, 1973-
        The very itchy bear / Nick Bland.
ISBN 978-1-4431-0495-1 (bound).--ISBN 978-1-4431-0496-8 (pbk.)
        1. Bears--Juvenile fiction. I. Title.

PZ10.3.B527Ve 2011   j823'.92   C2010-905020-7

First published by Scholastic Australia in 2010.
This edition published in Canada by Scholastic Canada Ltd. in 2011.
Copyright © 2010 by Nick Bland.

6 5 4 3 2 1   Printed in Singapore 46   11 12 13 14 15 16

Bear is here . . .

and here is Flea
(but Flea's a little small to see).

This is Flea about to bite,
but not because he's impolite.

He's biting Bear to say,

biting ^{high}

and

biting

low.

This is Flea **biting** Bear

under here

and over there.

Biting,

biting

everywhere!

SPLASH!

This is Bear
and this is Flea,

floating,

floating

out to sea.

This is Bear not quite sure
if Flea is with him any more.

This is Flea
reminding Bear . . .

that Flea has not gone anywhere.

This is Bear

flicking Flea

off his **fur** and

out to sea.

This is Bear
all alone,

frightened now he's on his own.

This is Bird

and this is Bear

and Flea is way, way

over there.

This is Flea
about to see
how scary hungry
birds can be!

This is Bear
in the sea
swimming fast to rescue Flea.

Flea is happy
Bear can swim.
This is Flea not biting him.

This is Flea
and this is Bear.

Together they go everywhere.